Five Minute

Bedtime Stories

Heart-warming
stories to read and share
at bedtime

Retold and illustrated by Kate Toms

make
believe
ideas

Contents

Twinkle, Twinkle, Little Star   4

Itsy Bitsy Spider   30

I Udderly Love You   56

10 Little Penguins   82

There was an Old Woman
who Lived in a Shoe   106

Hey Diddle Diddle   132

There was an Old Lady
who Swallowed a Fly   158

Lullabies   184

Twinkle Twinkle Little Star

Twinkle, twinkle,
little star,
how I wonder
what you are.

You **shine** above
the **world** so high,
like a **lightbulb**
in the **sky**.

I'd love to catch you
in my net . . .

8

and keep you as a special pet!

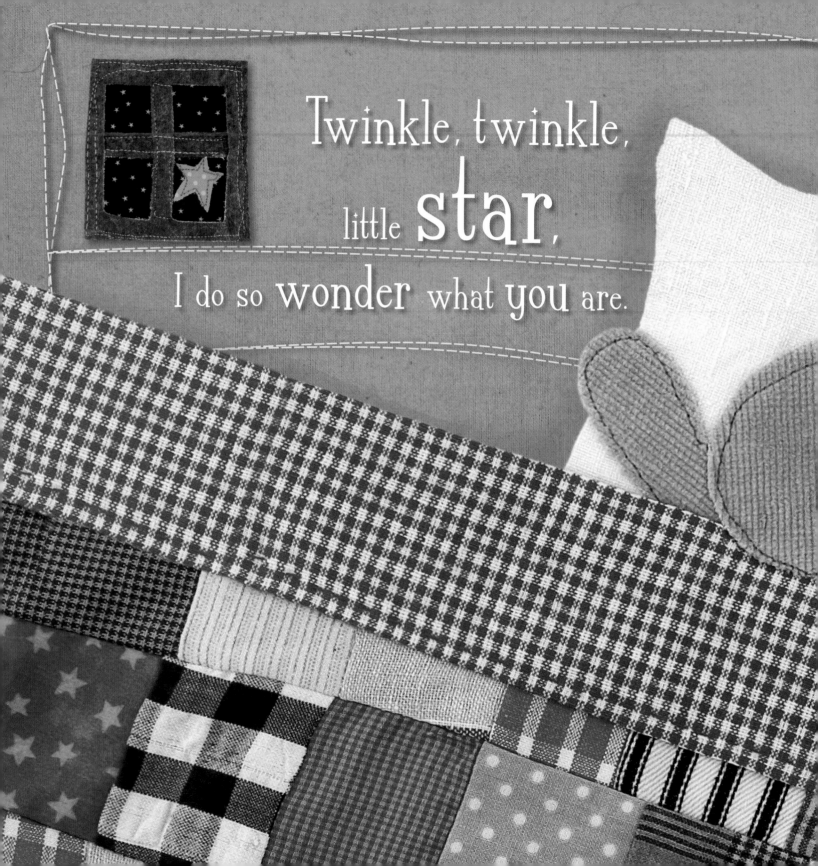

Twinkle, twinkle, little **star**, I do so **wonder** what **you** are.

When snuggled up in bed at night,

cozy, warm, and tucked up tight,

Z z z z Z

I dream that I can fly

a rocket . . .

5 4 3 2

and gather

stardust in my pocket.

13

Twinkle, twinkle little **star**, how I wonder what **you** are.

Does a **man** live on the **moon?**

14

Wait for me!

And did he see the dish and spoon?

And if the **moon**

Yummy!

is made of **cheese**,

will you save some for me, please?

Twinkle, twinkle, little star,
what do **you** see from afar?

Hello!

Hola!

Are there **mice** just like me
living way across the **sea?**

Guten Tag!

Bonjour!

Ciao!

Are there **stars** for us **all** up there?

All mine!

Wheeeeee!

20

Jump!

Or do some folks have to share?

Twinkle, twinkle, little **star**,
how I wonder
what **you** are!

When the **sky**
grows **dark** at **night**,
I **wish** and **wish**
with all my **might**

I want to be a **star** like you,

Wheeeeeeeee!

24

and see the world the way you do.

Twinkle, twinkle, little star,
how I wonder what you are.

When it's time to climb the stairs,

to **brush** my **teeth**
and say my **prayers,**

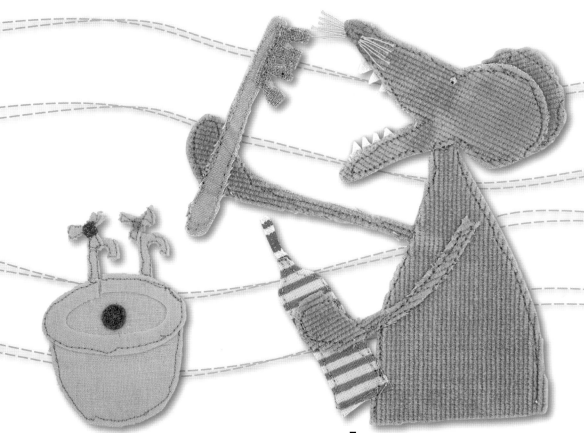

through my **window** I can see
that you are **smiling** down on me.

Twinkle, twinkle,
little **star**,
how I wonder
what **you** are.

Itsy Bitsy
spider

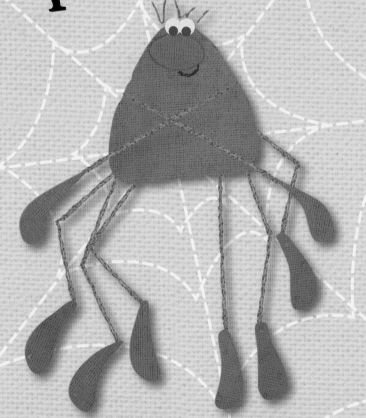

Itsy Bitsy
Spider

went **UP** the waterspout.

Down came the rain,
and washed the spider **out**.

Out came the SUN

and dried up all the rain,

so **Itsy Bitsy Spider**

climbed up the spout again.

Here we go again!

But why does Itsy climb the spout?

(In case you are in any doubt.)

Because he's SPUN his web up high,

so he can see the world go by . . .

(It's easy **dropping** to the floor,
but climbing **UP** is quite a chore.)

Itsy Bitsy Spider

doesn't like the **rain**,

he's got his **swimming** goggles on,

(he won't get caught again).

But . . . just as he starts climbing UP the waterspout, another shower of rain falls down and washes Itsy out!

Uh-oh!

Now **Itsy's** trying once again,

with **his** umbrella **ready**,

the **rain** won't beat him **this** time

if he takes it

nice and **steady**.

38

There **has** to be another way

to get home on a **rainy day!**

Looking **around**, what's **Itsy** seen?

A **round** and **bouncy** trampoline!

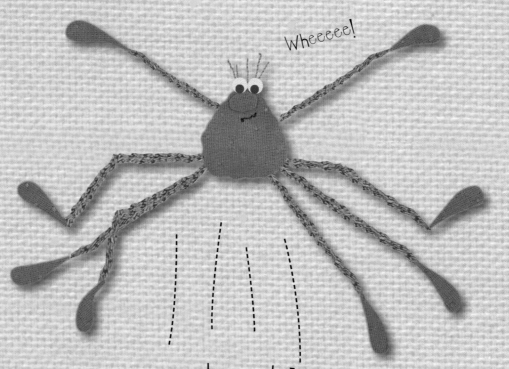

Wheeeee!

He's found a way to get home **fast** . . .

but bounces high

and flies straight past . . .

Not again!

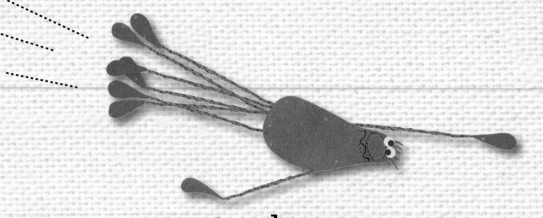

Over the hedge,
over the wall,
a blue striped tent
breaks his fall.

Looking puzzled,
Itsy thinks.
He rubs his hairy head and blinks.

The wash is **drying**,

the **weather's** fine,

44

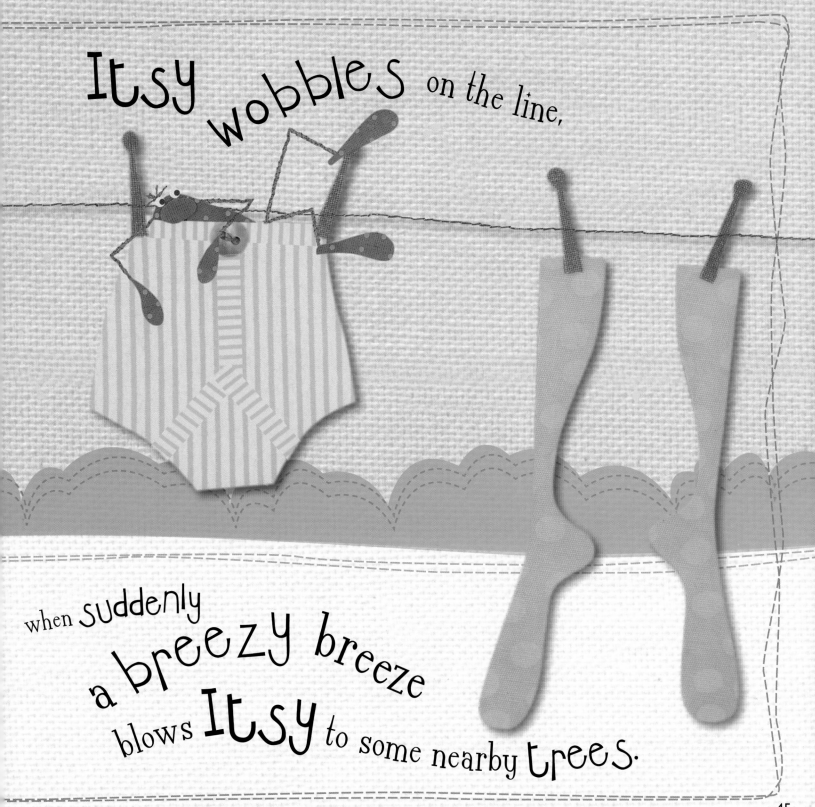

Itsy wobbles on the line, when suddenly a breezy breeze blows Itsy to some nearby trees.

Through the leaves,
Itsy spies
several pairs of
beady eyes.

"But **worse** than that,"
Itsy squeaks,

Itsy's running, all puffed out,

but in the distance,
sees the
spout.

49

It's the **best idea**
he's had **all day.**

He'll climb the spout **another way.**

The **rain** comes down

inside the spout,

so he'll climb UP

not IN, but out!

Back in his web,

he's happy now.

(It's easy when you've worked out how . . .)

The lesson learned?
Don't wear a frown—

even when the rain comes down!

So **Itsy Bitsy Spider**

can climb the waterspout.

And even if the **rain pours down**,

it can't wash **Itsy** out.

For **Itsy Bitsy Spider**

has found **another** way,

and now it's really easy

to climb the spout all day.

55

sque-e-eze!

sque-e-eze!

I love
everything about you:

Your tail, your ears, your toes.

I love the softness
of your skin,

your silky, s-moo-th, wet nose.

I love your every moo-vement,

the way you skip about,

and how your

hooves

point inwards,

while all your **knees** stick out!

I love the way
you chatter,
the funny things you say,
the moo-sic
that you sing to me,

the silly games we play.

And when you
go exploring,

tweet! tweet!

DoG

it makes me really proud,

Grrr!
Grrr!

to know you'll always find me,

even in a crowd.

At nighttime, in the **moo**-nlight, when the stars shine overhead,

I watch you as you're sleeping
in your snuggly, little bed.

ha-ha!
ha-ha!

I love you when you're happy,

I love you when you're sad. moo-hoo!

Even when you're **moo**-dy,

not meaning to be bad.

Every day with you is special,
I love you
through and through,

I UDDERLY, UDDERLY LOVE YOU
and I know you love me too!

10 LITTLE PENGUINS

10 little penguins are

but **1** of them has lost her

Where's Pamela?

84

ready for some fun . . .

way before the day's begun.

Search me!

85

9 playful penguins are

bouncing really high . . .

1 penguin jumps too far and zooms up to the sky!

bake a tasty cake . . .

1 penguin eats too fast and now has tummy ache!

Oh dear!

6 happy penguins, all

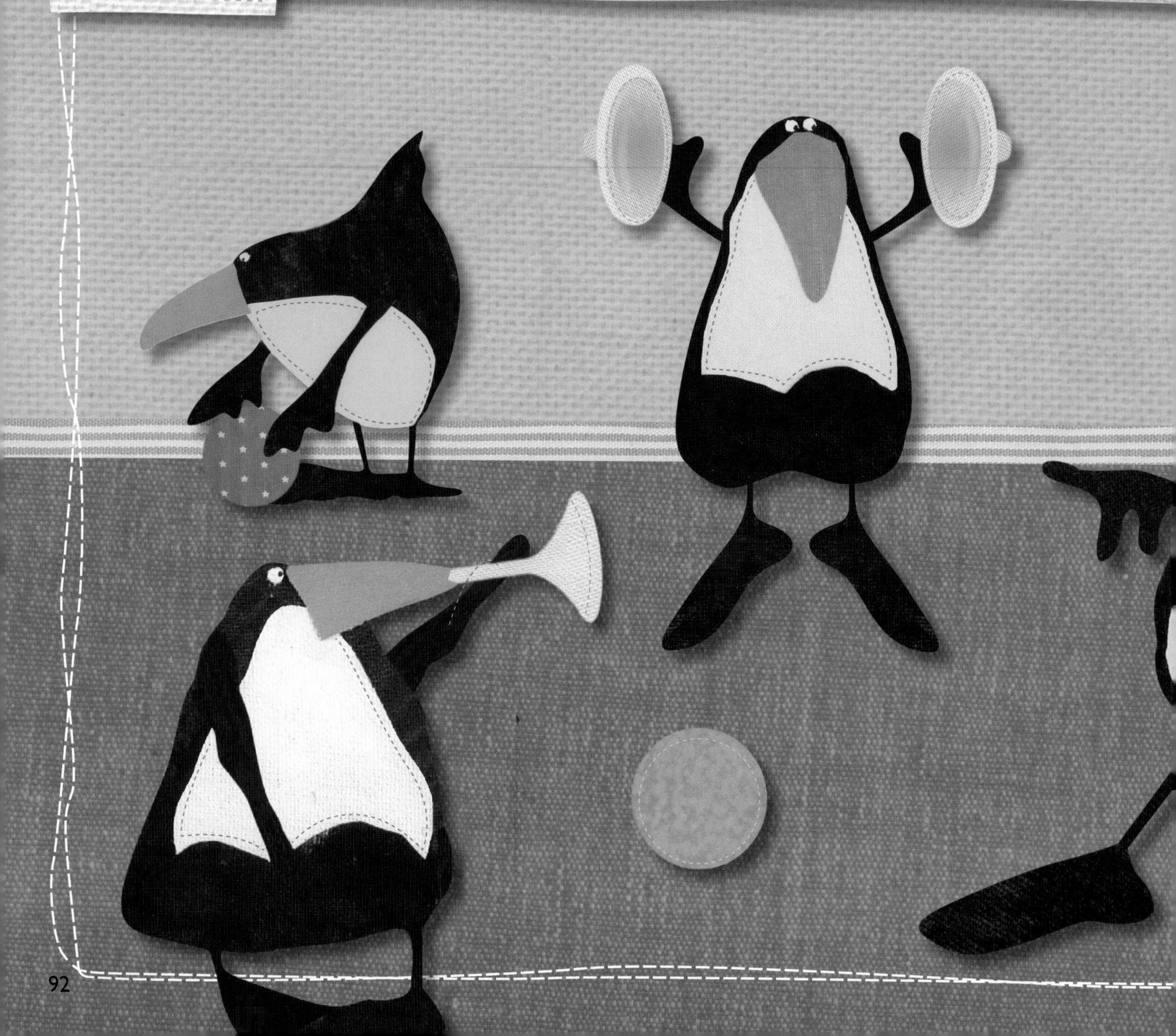

1 of them decides to leave;
she doesn't like the noise.

quiet penguins watch

but 1 has seen this one before

their favorite show . . .

and thinks it's time to go.

1 cries, "Not sardines!" and jump

Keep it smoooooth!

1 tries

a somersault

and crashes

to the ground!

a bubble bath . . .

1 slips on a bar of soap, and makes the other laugh!

1 tired little penguin.

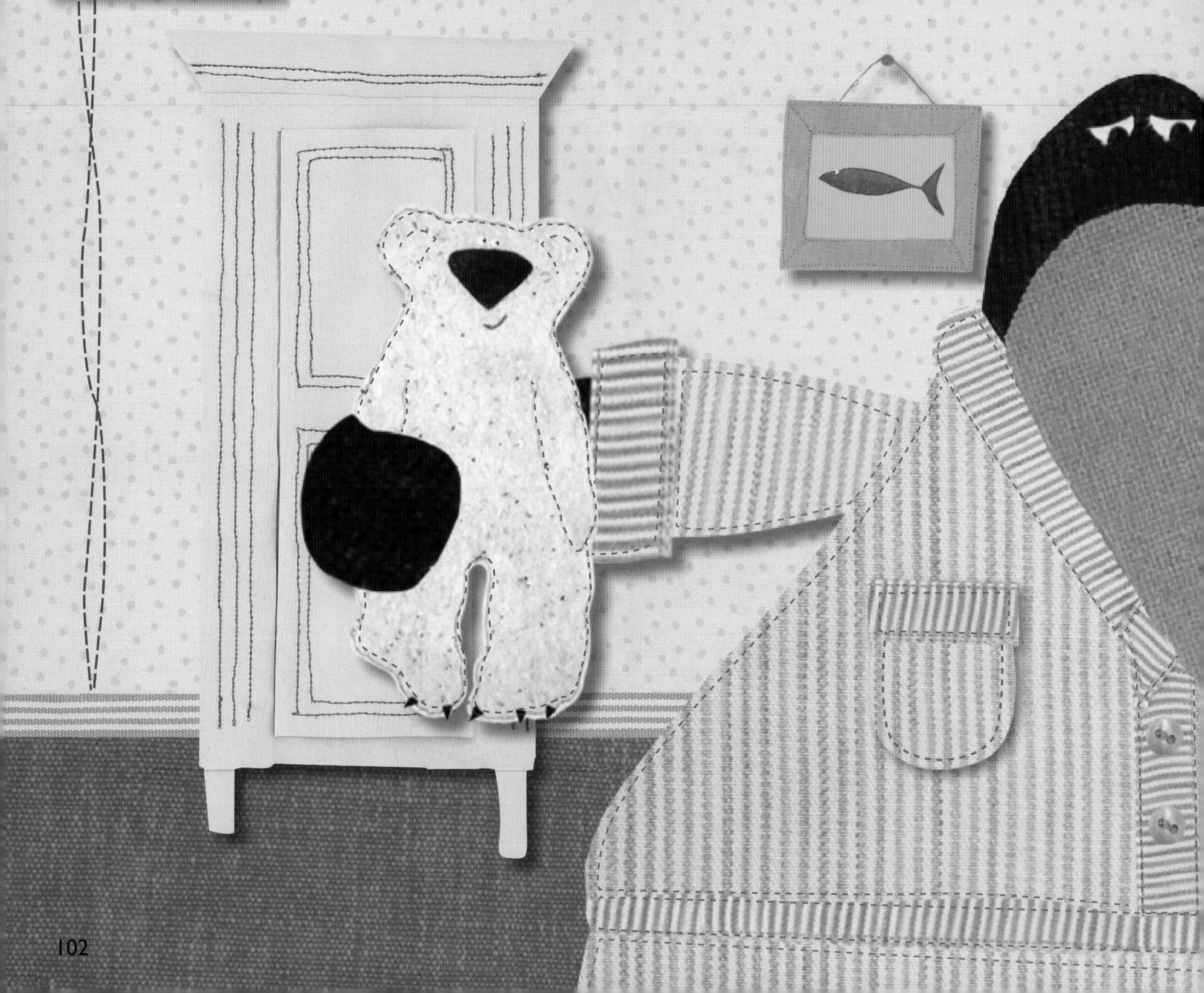

What a sleepyhead!

Yawn!

had all gone home . . .

But look!
They're in her bed!

There was an old woman who lived in a shoe

There was an **old woman** who lived in a **shoe**,

with so many **children** —

what could they all do?

Every day, they'd have some fun,

but not until

the **chores** were done!

On **Monday,** they have clothes to wash,

and sheets to clean

with a **splish** and a **splosh.**

Spinning around in the **big** machine, the laundry is soon all fresh and clean.

soapso

Now watch them **pull** with all their might —

they've tied the laundry to their **kite!**

There was an **old woman**
who lived in a **shoe,**
with so many **children**
and **so much** to do.

On **Tuesday,** every child **must** choose
some polish and a pair of shoes.
They **scrape** and **brush** and **polish** hard,
in a line out in the yard.

Later on, they go for a **swim,**
put armbands on, and **JUMP** right in!

They **laugh** and **dive**
and **splash about**

and towels are **ready**
when they get out.

There was an **old woman** who lived in a **shoe,**
with so many **children** — how the time **flew!**

On **Wednesday,** they get on their **knees**
to pick some **carrots, beans,** and **peas** —
there's lots of **digging,** gathering **berries,**
and **filling bowls** with piles of **cherries!**
Then . . .

It's **music time** for girls and boys,

lots of singing, lots of **noise!**

They **dance** and **sing** and twirl around

and make a really **amazing** sound.

On **Thursday,** a trip to the vet's

Once they are **home,** they brush the **fur.**

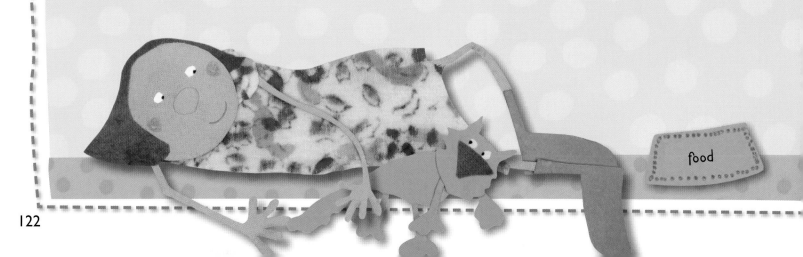

food

to get a checkup for the **pets.**

vet

Listen to the **kittens purrr!**

milk

On **Friday,** it's off to the **park** to play –
a **happy** way to spend the day.

A **picnic's** packed, the stroller's full —
and don't forget
the **bouncy** ball!

By **Saturday,** the cupboard's **bare.**
The **old woman** sits in her **chair**

to make a **list** of things they need,

with so many **hungry** mouths to feed!

A **shopping** trip
is quickly planned,
and **everybody**
lends a hand.

Soon the **cart** is

piled high

with all the things

they need to **buy.**

Sunday is the day of rest –
see them in their
Sunday best,

all in a **row**, **one** by **one**.

Can you **remember**

the **things** they've done?

the cow

jumps over

the Moon,

the little dog laughs
to see
such fun,

and the dish
runs away
with the spoon.

when Cat plays his fiddle, Dog sings along to the tune,

Cow's in the bath,

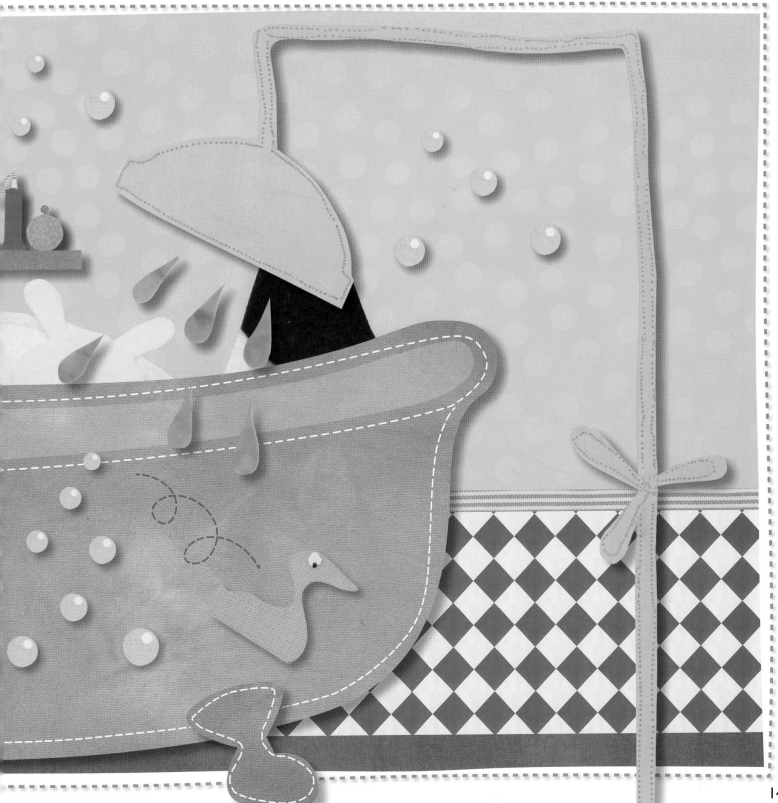

then Dog starts to **laugh**

when Dish comes back with the spoon.

The piggies all prance,

the elephants dance,

the monkeys start

softly to croon,

149

and, hand
in hand,
the kangaroos
stand,

tapping their toes to the tune!

Hey diddle diddle,

Cat hangs up
his fiddle
and Moon looks down
from on high.

and everyone's waving bye-bye, bye-bye,

and everyone's waving bye-bye.

There was an **old lady** who **swallowed** a fly. Why, oh **why,** did she swallow a **fly?**

Oh my, oh my!

Tra la la!

That little old lady was **walking** along, enjoying the sunshine and **singing** a song.

When **all of the sudden** a fly flew south . . .

and ended up **flying**

right into her **mouth!**

That **poor** old lady – what a to-do!

Imagine if that happened

to **you!**

The fly now buzzes and tickles her tummy (she didn't think it tasted so yummy)!

But suddenly she has an idea to make the naughty fly disappear:

to catch the fly she swallows a spider —

so now she has them both inside her!

Oh my, oh my!

Down by the pond
she **spots** a **frog**,

sitting still on a speckled log.

Without even saying,

"How do you do?"

she picks up the frog and

swallows

him too!

cRoAK!

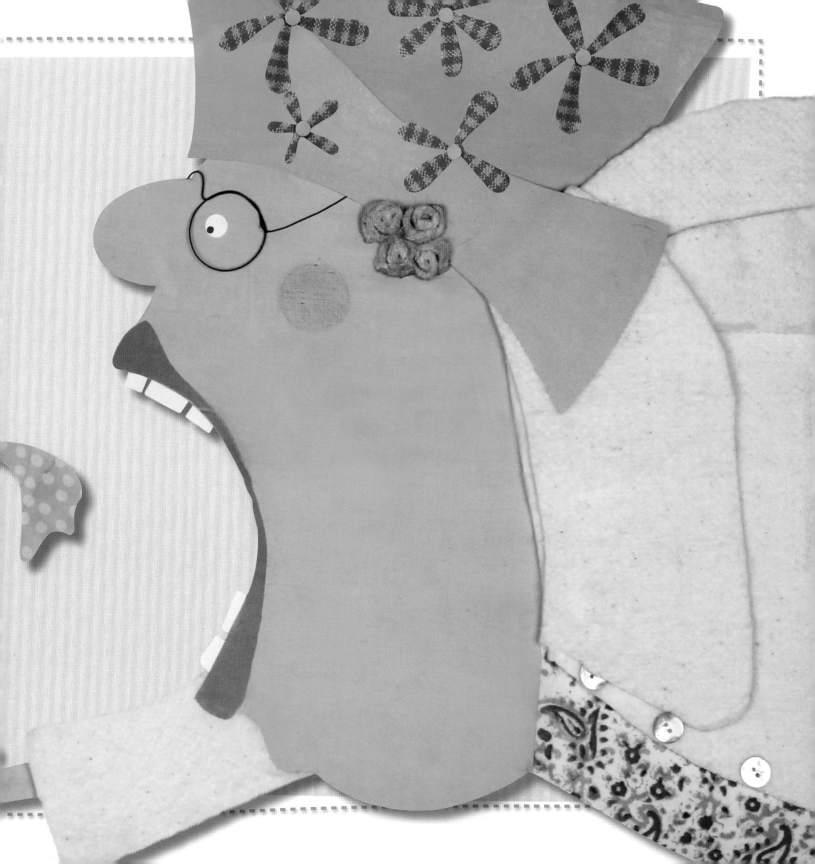

Feeling just a **little** **queasy**

(certainly not so bright and breezy),

she **spots** a heron on a nest –

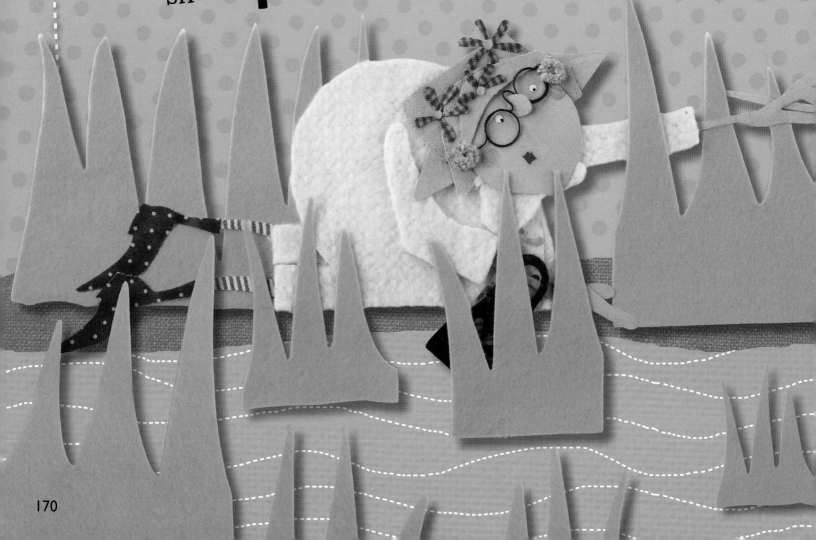

I wonder if **YOU** can **guess** the rest?

How **absurd**...

to swallow a **bird!**

Oh my, oh my!

How could she **do** that?
We don't know how —
but you won't **believe**
what happens now . . .

Pretty Kitty
sits and **purrs**;
from behind her something **stirs.**

Before **poor puss**

has time

to flee . . .

she's washed down
with a
cup of
tea!

Imagine **that,**
to swallow a **cat!**

Oh my, oh my!

By this time it's **getting dark.**
Prince the **dog** plays in the **park.**

But poor old Prince
just does not see
the **old lady**
lurking by a big tree.

GULP!

Poor Prince . . .

The old lady's **tummy** is about to **burst** – she wishes she'd thought more **carefully** first.

She swallowed the **dog**
to catch the cat.
She swallowed the **cat**
to catch the bird.
She swallowed the **bird**
to catch the frog.
She swallowed the **frog**
to catch the spider.
She swallowed the **spider**
to catch the fly . . .

if **only** that fly had just **flown by.**

Oh my, oh my!

Lavender's blue

Lavender's blue, dilly, dilly,
lavender's green.
When you are king, dilly, dilly,
I shall be queen.
Who told you so, dilly, dilly,
who told you so?
'Twas my own heart, dilly, dilly,
that told me so.

I see the moon

I see the moon
and the moon sees me.
God bless the moon
and God bless me.

Sleep, Baby, sleep

Sleep, Baby, sleep,
long and safe and deep.
The wind will blow
the dreamland tree
and from it shake
sweet dreams for thee.
Sleep, Baby, sleep,
our cottage vale is deep.
The little lamb
is on the green,
with snowy fleece
so soft and clean.
Sleep, Baby, sleep.

Rock-a-bye, Baby

Rock-a-bye, Baby,
on the treetop.
When the wind blows,
the cradle will rock.
When the bough breaks,
the cradle will fall,
and down will come Baby,
cradle and all.